MERMAIDS
DON'T HAVE POCKETS

BY TIM RADES

To my Lil Peanut, Presley

SO YOU'D LIKE TO BE A MERMAID

AND SWIM AROUND SO FREE.

LET ME TELL YOU THAT A MERMAID'S LIFE
IS NOT ALL IT SEEMS TO BE.

SURE WE CAN SWIM FROM DUSK 'TIL DAWN

AND NOT ONCE COME UP FOR AIR.

OUR FRIENDS ARE FISH AND WHALES AND CLAMS

AND SHARKS IF WE SO DARE.

WE EAT ALL TYPES OF FUNNY THINGS

EVERY NIGHT AND EVERY DAY.

WE SLEEP IN COMFY CLAM SHELLS

BY THE LIGHT OF EELS AND RAYS.

OUR HAIR FLOATS IN THE WATER

AND FORGET ABOUT DEODORANT

WE NEVER HAVE TO CARE.

BUT UNDER THE SEA IS NOT ENTIRELY

WHAT IT SEEMS TO BE,

BECAUSE THERE IS A GREAT ADVANTAGE

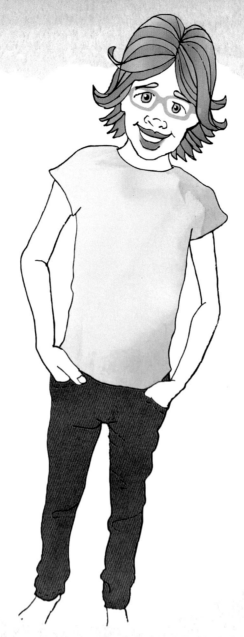

FOR HUMAN GIRLS, YOU'LL SEE.

MERMAIDS DON'T HAVE POCKETS.

I KNOW THAT SOUNDS SO SIMPLE.

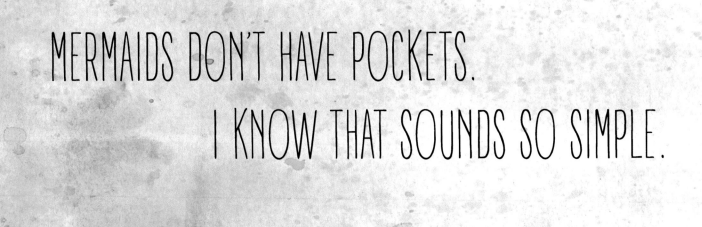

BUT I CAN SHOW YOU JUST HOW BIG THAT IS WITH JUST A FEW EXAMPLES.

WE DON'T HAVE A PLACE TO CARRY CASH

OR EVEN KEEP SPARE CHANGE,

OR WEAR PANTS
TO SUPPORT OUR FAVORITE TEAM
THE DAY OF THE BIG GAME,

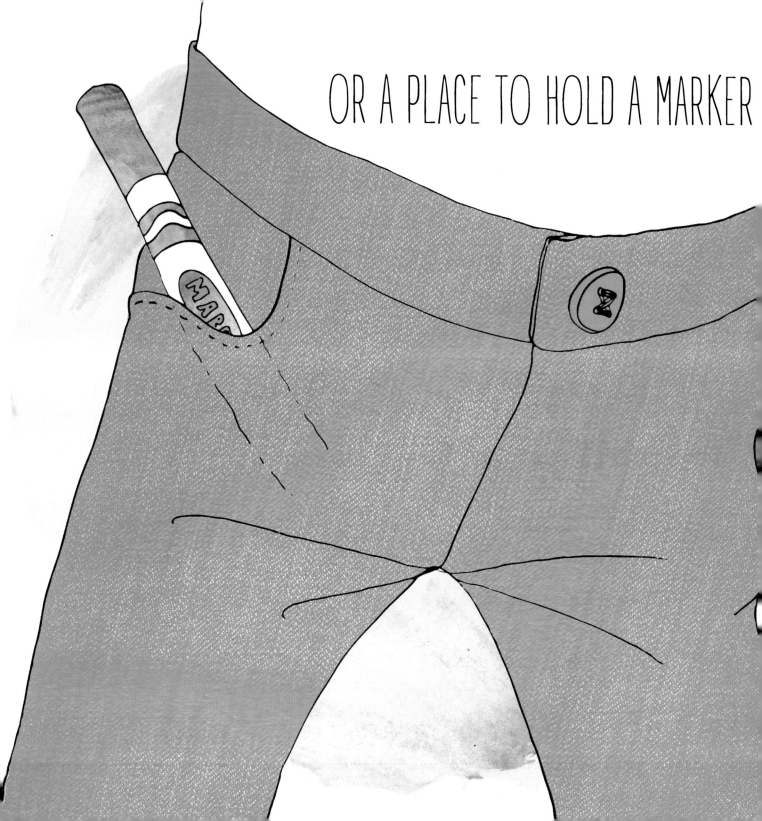

OR A PLACE TO HOLD A MARKER

OR HOLD OUR GREEN SMART PHONE,

OR PUT OUR HANDS TO STRIKE A POSE,

OR STORE TICKETS FOR A SHOW,

NO POCKETS TO OVERDECORATE,

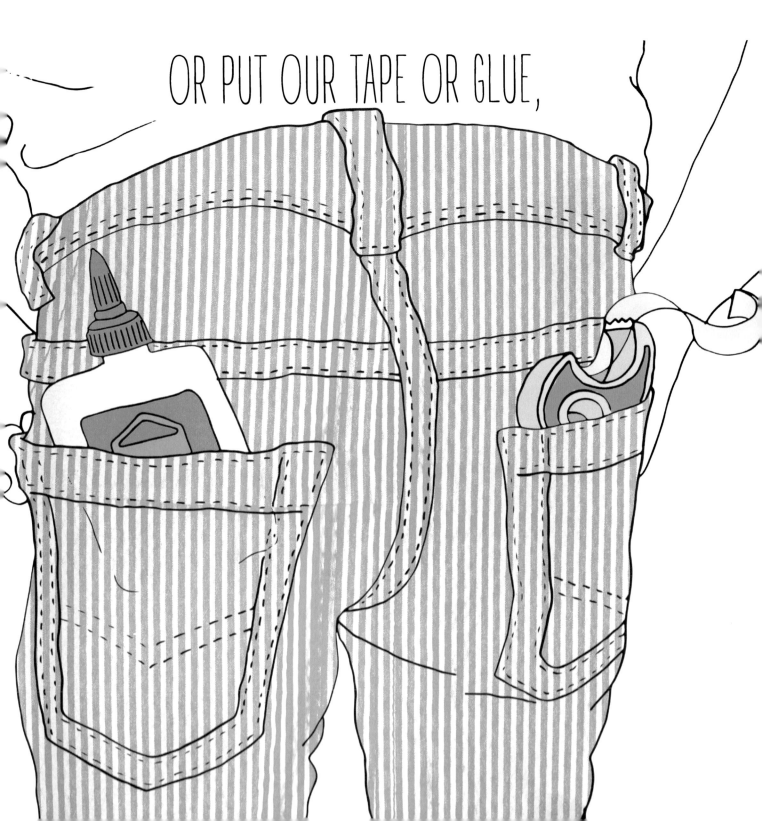

OR PUT OUR TAPE OR GLUE,

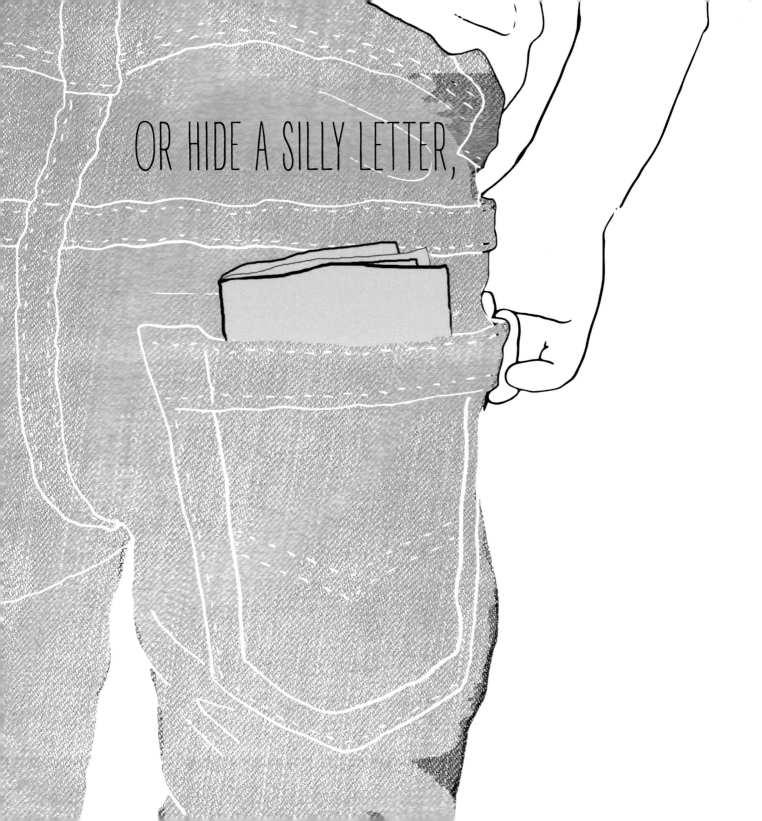

FOR OUR BEST FRIEND AT SCHOOL.

OR KEEP A SNACK FOR LATER,

THAT CALLS SLUGS AND ALLIGATORS.

SIMPLY ENJOY THE THINGS YOU HAVE

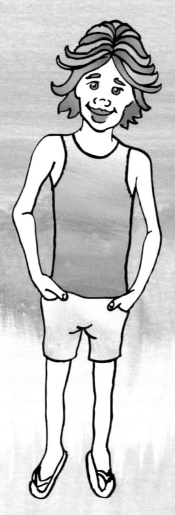

ON LAND OR BY THE SEA.

SO BE THE VERY
BESTEST
YOU
THAT
YOU
COULD EVER BE

BECAUSE SOME MERMAIDS

WISH THAT THEY HAD LEGS

SO THEY COULD BE LIKE YOU.

SO REALIZE JUST WHAT YOU ARE

Made in the USA
San Bernardino, CA
22 May 2020